"How are you going to make Mr. Fuzzypants come back to life?" I demanded at breakfast on Wednesday morning. Mercedes wasn't at the table yet, so I figured it was time for Dad to spill.

"I'm going to do some magic," he said matter-of-factly.

I studied his face, awaiting some conspiratorial wink or something. "Can I help?"

"No. This is tricky." He wasn't meeting my eyes, and I didn't like it one bit.

"A spell?" I repeated, emphasizing the disbelief in my voice. "Yes."

"Dad, I helped you and Mom convince Misty that Santa and the Easter Bunny still exist. I know there's no real magic."

He gave me a pointed look and glanced nervously at the entrance into the kitchen to make sure my sister hadn't overheard that. "There *is* real magic. It's just not for children."

"I'm hardly a child!"

Other Fiction and Poetry by Trisha J. Wooldridge

Mirror of Hearts

"Family Reunion," in *Demonic Visions 6*

"Oprah Funds 'End of the World' Project in Memory of Savant Child Author," in *Demonic Visions 5*

"Steadfast in the Face of Zombies," in *Once Upon an Apocalypse Volume 1*

"Fixed," in *Corrupts Absolutely?*

"The Crocodile Below," *Wicked Tales*

"The Widow Mills," *Wicked Seasons*

"Kali's Promise," in *Epitaphs*

With Christy Tohara

"Last Gate to Faerie," in *Bad-Ass Faeries: In All Their Glory*

"Party Crashers," in *Bad-Ass Faeries: Just Plain Bad*

TEA
WITH
MR. FUZZYPANTS

TRISHA J. WOOLDRIDGE

Pole to Pole Publishing
Baltimore

Tea with Mr. Fuzzypants
Copyright ©2016 by Trisha J. Wooldridge
All Rights Reserved

To my dearest Scott, thank you for putting up with all the evil bunnies. And being an awesome husband.

To Miss Rhetta, Lady Anne, Loki, Cameron, and Vash, thank you for teaching me your evil ways.

TEA
WITH
MR. FUZZYPANTS

*M*ercedes's howling scream yanked my dad's and my attention away from our cookies and milk. We shared a look of fear and dashed out the back door toward the bunny hutch.

My eighteen-year-old big sister knelt on the soggy ground, rocking back and forth like she did during any meltdown, her broad face scrunched, bright red, and smeared with dirt and tears. She was inside the fold-up pen set up for Mr. Fuzzypants, a brown and white Dutch Lop Dad had won for her about seven Big E fairs ago. I was still in a stroller then, and I got booted out so Mom could rig bungee cords to attach the bunny cage to it; I had to walk the whole rest of the day.

"Daddy, Daddy, Daddy, Mr. Fuzzypants isn't moving! He's all hard, like a rock! Do something, Daddy!" Mercedes sobbed, her cradling arms revealing brown and white fur and the glassy eyes of the decidedly not moving Mr. Fuzzypants.

"Oh, sweetheart." Dad knelt beside Mercedes and wrapped his arms around her shoulders. I could see tears in his eyes as he rocked with her.

I leaned against the corner of the house, poked my toe in a leftover pile of snow, and did my best not to look annoyed. I felt bad for my sister; I really did. She loved that stupid rabbit like nothing else. But this was *my* time with Dad. Mercedes needs all sorts of special help. I get that, and I get that it's not her fault, but Mom and Dad always had to spend extra time with her. A few years ago, I got especially angry about it—even though I knew it wasn't anyone's fault—and I started "acting out". At least, that's how the school psychologist described it. Mom, Dad, and I had a meeting, and they started setting aside time just for me. On Sunday afternoons and after school on days when Dad hadn't worked the night before, he and I would have snacks and throw around a ball or Frisbee, or we'd go for a hike or something. Anything that was just us. Mercedes would take care of her rabbit and do things with Mom, and it all worked out.

Then, Mom fell down the stairs and broke her neck a few months ago, just after Christmas. Now it's just Dad and us two girls.

But Dad still tried. He made a schedule—schedules help Mercedes a lot—and he set her bunny time every day after school. During Mercedes's "bunny time," I had my Dad time. We still had to stay near "in case of emergencies" with Mercedes, but it was still *our* time.

I didn't *want* to be angry or upset. I felt really bad for my big sister—who I'd also been helping "take care of" for as long as I could remember—because I knew she loved Mr. Fuzzypants. But, seriously, did the dumb bunny *really* have to choose *now* to go and die on my sister? Stupid rabbit.

"No! It's not fair! God can't take Mommy and Mr. Fuzzypants both! I want him back!" Mercedes was all but yelling in Dad's ear. She was nearly as tall as Mom, so even while Dad was holding her, her mouth was right by his head.

Damn the dumb bunny. *I* wanted Mom back. I knew having a fit wouldn't change being dead, no matter how hard I *wanted* it or cried about it, and I was only ten.

I gritted my teeth. As grown-up as Mercedes might look, couldn't *get* how I felt, at least not right now—and who knows if she ever would. It's so frustrating to want to be angry at someone and know you shouldn't be. It's so unfair.

I must have been steaming despite my best efforts because Dad caught my eye. "I'm sorry, Portia," he mouthed while rocking my sister. "I'll make it up to you. Promise."

I nodded, knowing better than to bet on the promise. I didn't doubt my Dad's intention; I *know* he wanted to make me feel better. The problem was that Mercedes *needed* him more. And now he was just one parent.

"I've got homework." I was rather proud of how caring I made my voice sound as I added, "I'm sorry about Mr. Fuzzypants, Misty."

My consolation only seemed to make her sob and yell into Dad's shoulder even harder. Dad and I shared a nod, and I retreated into the house to get my reading assignment done.

*M*ercedes remained inconsolable over Mr. Fuzzypants. *It* was almost worse than when Mom died, except in the sense of Dad's work—where it *was* worse. Walmart, where he did night stocking, let him take time off with pay when Mom died. No one gives you time off for your daughter's dead pet, though. When Mercedes wouldn't let up on her meltdown and wouldn't go to school the next day, he didn't get any sleep before his third shift...and she was still in full meltdown when I came back from school, so he had to call out of work.

He totally forgot to call Miss Carrie, our night-time nanny, and cancel, though. When she let herself in after we'd had dinner, Mercedes started screaming all over again because Dad had promised he wasn't going to work, but Miss Carrie was here, and that meant he was going to work, and *wah wah wah*.

I started loading the dishwasher to get away from my ear-splitting sister. Dad was grateful for my helpfulness, so score one for me being the *good daughter*.

Miss Carrie, who has a special license to nanny for special needs kids, helped Dad calm Mercedes and get her to bed. When a full half-hour passed without any wails (and I had finished pretty much the rest of the week's homework), I returned to the living room where an embarrassed-looking Dad was letting out Miss Carrie and apologizing.

"…I'm just going to take the rest of the week off, but here's for coming out tonight. It's just…" Dad passed her a handful of cash, brow furrowed.

"I understand, Mr. Cartwright." She nodded, though she took the money he was handing her. "Times are tight for all of us. But I understand you have to be extra careful…" Her blue eyes darted toward me. With a smile, she continued, "Call me whenever you're ready. Have a good night, Portia!"

"Good night, Miss Carrie."

She wasn't a bad nanny, and she did try to make time for me, but Dad had hired her mostly *because* of my sister. If it was just me, he could hire any old nanny for probably much less money. Not only am I not "special needs," but I'm pretty self-sufficient for my age—probably for someone even older than me.

Dad knew that I'd overheard the conversation. As soon as he shut the door, he swept me into his arms, carrying me like the knight carries the rescued princess in storybooks. Not that I ever intended to need rescue, but I couldn't stop from smiling as he held me and kissed the top of my head.

"Everything's gonna be okay, Luxury Car Number Two."

I stuck my tongue out at him. "I'm not a car. I'm a girl. Actually, I'm a moon and a Shakespeare character because you said so."

Mom's job—and love—had been fixing cars. She used to be the only woman mechanic at one of the top fix-it places in the city. In her spare time, she used to buy, fix, and resell old cars. I had been *this close* to being named Porsche, but Dad had changed the letters. Mom had been the one to nickname me and my sister Luxury Car Number Two and Luxury Car Number One. Yeah, my mom was weird, but I missed the weird parts the most, and I'm pretty sure Dad did, too.

In fact, one of Mom's projects was still in our garage, making Dad have to park in the driveway. My Uncle James's '76 Mustang. She'd gotten it last fall, but it had needed a lot of work; she died before she finished fixing it up. Mr. Murray, one of the guys who used to work with Mom, kept calling about buying it from us, even though it still needed all that work.

Dad had been ignoring his calls. I couldn't blame him, though, even with tight money. Sometimes I still snuck into the garage and sat in the driver's seat, pretending I was listening to Mom tell me all the stuff she was doing. I used to help with all her projects. I was her best "assistant mechanic," she always said.

When I grow up, I'll be the best "mechanic," and not just an assistant. Like Mom was. That's what I think of when I don't want to think about missing her.

With Mercedes asleep, I had Dad all to myself. He let me stay up to watch four episodes of *My Little Pony* while we snuggled under my Apple Jack fleece blanket.

*A*ll the things got even worse than when after Mom died. Because of dead Mr. Fuzzypants.

It was stupid, and I hated it, but Mercedes was melting down even more about her dumb bunny dying. I wanted to slap her across the face because moms are way more important than bunnies, but that would have made things even harder for Dad. He couldn't even go to work because my sister was such a mess. And I knew that if Dad couldn't go to work, we wouldn't have any money.

Even at my age, you know how important having enough money is.

One of Dad's work friends, a man named Kelly, brought over a "new" bunny for Mercedes, but that made things worse.

"He's just like another Mr. Fuzzypants," Kelly—who I called Mr. Ditmars out loud, though I really wanted to call a guy "Kelly"—

said. I could've told him that wasn't the best thing to say, but it's not like grown-ups generally listen to ten-year-olds.

Mercedes's face started getting red, and her lips stuck out and began to pop and sputter as she formed angry words. "He-he-he... he's *not* another Mister Fuzzypants! There can never be another Mister Fuzzypants!" Her eyes started to get brighter and she slapped the bunny carrier so hard there was a little dent and crack in the cheap plastic. "The color! His pants aren't dark enough. And he's not the right size. It's *not* Mister Fuzzypants! You can't just replace Mister Fuzzypants!"

Kelly snatched up the travel cage in just enough time to avoid Mercedes hitting it again. Inside, the Not-Mister-Fuzzypants gave a loud *thump* that nearly knocked the carrier out of Kelly's arms.

It's a creepy feeling when I see adults, like Mr. Kelly Ditmars (who was even bigger and taller than Dad) back away, scared, from my sister. Dad put an arm around Mercedes to comfort her, as well as hopefully keep her from lashing out at anything else.

"Sorry, Hank," Kelly said to my dad, continuing to get closer to the door as he hugged the carrier to his chest. "I was just trying to help..."

"I know, Kelly," my dad said, rubbing Mercedes's back as she sobbed. "Thank you...and explain to Bucknam...you know."

"I will. Good luck, man. Bye, Portia." He gave me an apologetic wave too.

I waved back, happy someone had noticed me just a little.

After *that* mess, things only got worse. Mercedes wouldn't even let Dad sleep, much less go to work. Whenever she didn't see him, she'd start a tantrum.

In fact, I think my sister broke my dad's brain. After a Friday with her waking up almost every hour screaming, followed by clinging to him *all* weekend, he finally got her to fall asleep by promising, if she was very good and let him go to work Sunday night, he'd invite Mr. Fuzzypants back to life for a tea party on Wednesday, after his Tuesday off.

"**H**ow are you going to make Mr. Fuzzypants come back to life?" I demanded at breakfast on Wednesday morning. Mercedes wasn't at the table yet, so I figured it was time for Dad to spill. I had patiently waited since Saturday night for him to let me in on some plan to trick my sister or something. With an afternoon tea threatening *any* Dad time for me since Thursday night, I'd just about lost my patience.

"I'm going to do some magic," he said matter-of-factly.

I studied his face, awaiting some conspiratorial wink or something. "Can I help?"

"No. This is tricky." He wasn't meeting my eyes, and I didn't like it one bit.

"A spell?" I repeated, emphasizing the disbelief in my voice.

"Yes."

"Dad, I helped you and Mom convince Misty that Santa and the Easter Bunny still exist. I know there's no real magic."

He gave me a pointed look and glanced nervously at the entrance into the kitchen to make sure my sister hadn't overheard that. "There *is* real magic. It's just not for children."

"I'm hardly a child!"

Dad was clearly amused by what I felt was a statement of fact. I gave him half-credit for at least trying to hide his smile. Only half, though.

"I'm very adult for my age. My teachers say so. And definitely more adult than Misty, and she's eighteen!"

"That's not very nice to say, Portia." My dad spoke softly, giving me a frown.

I glowered at him. "It's not nice to think the fact that I'm mature and helpful and smart is funny, either."

His lips twitched. "I'm sorry, sweetie. Yes, you are mature for your age. And very smart. Too smart, sometimes." He reached across the table and tweaked my nose. I don't know what it is, but there's something about getting your nose tweaked or poked that makes you smile no matter how annoyed you are. As I tried to fight the smile, he explained, "This spell is something only one person can do. It's going to take a lot of concentration for me to do it. Can you please understand that?"

I sighed but nodded.

"Good." He reached over and kissed me.

"So, where did you learn this magic?" I was still pretty sure there wasn't any actual magic involved, but I wanted to know what was going on.

The phone started ringing, and I saw dad narrow his eyes at it. He continued cutting up the French toast for Mercedes. She liked it in small pieces and not hot. With each ring, he glared even more—but didn't go answer it. Finally, the answering machine—yes, my family still has an old-school answering machine—picked up and it was Mr. Murry. Again. "Hey, Hank, I, um, I was just wondering about picking up the Mustang. I know it's, uh, your morning off, so I figured you'd be, uh, free. And if you want any help with anything around the house, I might be, uh, able to help. Uh...gimme a call..."

Dad's chopping seemed to get even louder through the message. He snorted when it was done and went to pour himself another cup of coffee. When it was clear he must have forgotten about my question, I repeated myself. "So, where did you learn the 'real' magic? For the tea party?"

After another long pause, he finally muttered, "James helped me."

"Uncle James? Who's in jail?" Whose car Mr. Murry kept calling about? I glanced at the answering machine. Out of the corner of my eye, I saw him glare again in that direction too.

"Yes." My dad's voice got an edge to it, the one I knew meant he didn't want me to ask any more questions.

While I did pause, something feeling funny in my stomach, I ignored that edge as I usually did. "If Uncle James knows magic, why doesn't he use it to get out of jail? You said that he was wasn't really guilty of…whatever he did…" (Mom and Dad never actually told me what he did, except it had to do with drugs—which are bad—and someone getting killed, but not by Uncle James.) "…and he had only been trying to help." Whatever actually happened, it happened just after he dropped his car off for Mom to fix, right when school had started back, and it was something BIG. All the kids recognized our parents' names in the paper because they had to testify. I was *so* picked on because I didn't talk about it. Mom and Dad had been *very specific* to Mercedes and me that we shouldn't talk about *anything* related to Uncle James to *anyone*. I continued to offer my thoughts even as I saw Dad gritting his teeth. "Maybe Uncle James should've used magic to not get arrested or to make it so you and Mom didn't have to go testify in court. That would've been helpful."

"The magic doesn't work that way," he said, jaw still clenched. Then he closed his eyes and took a deep breath, like what Mercedes's therapists tell all of us to do when we're getting frustrated. He continued, a little calmer, "This is a special kind of magic."

"Magic? We're doing magic?" My sister's eyes lit up as she came in for breakfast. She was wearing a pretty flowered dress, and her wavy brown hair was in two long ponytails with blue bows because she wasn't sure she'd have time to change for the tea party when she got home from school.

I rolled my eyes. "Dad's doing magic so we can have tea with Mr. Fuzzypants this afternoon." I let my voice reveal exactly how much I believed that statement.

Dad gave me an even more scolding look, but as I expected, my tone was utterly lost on my sister. "It's going to be a magic tea party! Just like *Alice in Wonderland*. Will there be cake? And cookies?"

"Yes, there will be cake and cookies, Misty, but remember, this is a *secret* tea party. You can't talk about it. Not in front of anyone, remember?"

Just like everything related to Uncle James, I thought to myself.

Dad emphasized, because you have to make everything *very* clear for Mercedes. "If you talk about it, the magic might not work to get Mr. Fuzzypants here."

My sister nodded vigorously and made a zipper motion across her mouth, and then a twisting and tossing motion to show her lips were locked and the key was thrown away.

I rolled my eyes again but managed to keep my mouth shut for the rest of breakfast.

My after-school Dad-Time was turning into tea with an undead bunny. Oh. Yay.

Mercedes and I went to *different schools, so we took* different buses. My bus stop was a few blocks away and Mercedes got let off in front of my house, where I always met her, and we walked inside together.

With only the two of us, Mercedes felt safe enough to patter on about what kind of tea rabbits would drink and if Dad was making carrot cake. She didn't like carrot cake, but she was sure Mr. Fuzzypants would since he loved it when she fed him carrots. I *mn-hm*ed and half-listened as I usually did while we walked to the front door. My mind was busy trying to figure out what Dad was planning and how he would make a dead bunny come back to life.

And a teensy, tiny little part of my brain wondered, just a little bit, if he really was going to do magic.

And an even teensier part of that tiny part wondered, if he *could* do that kind of magic, why didn't he bring Mom back?

Another not-so-tiny thought tickled my brain, too. We didn't have a funeral or anything for Mr. Fuzzypants. I mean, I read about pet funerals and saw them on TV. They're nothing big, just a family digging a hole in the ground, putting the pet's body in a decorated box or blanket, saying some prayers, then filling up the hole and putting some marker there. Not that I really cared about the stupid rabbit, but the fact we hadn't done that didn't sit well with me.

Silence interrupted my thoughts. I looked at Mercedes, who was staring at me with her reddish-brown eyes. "Mahogany," Dad called them, same color as Mom's eyes. Her young-looking face in her grown-up sized head expressed she was waiting for something.

"I don't know?" That usually covered most questions people ask when I wasn't paying attention.

"You should've dressed up for school, like I did. I don't want us to be late if we have to wait for you to get dressed up."

I looked down at my jeans and softball T-shirt. "I think I look fine" was all I had time to say. Dad met us at the door with a big smile and ushered us into the kitchen. There was a fancy glass teapot, already steaming on the table. The *good* plates, the ones that usually only came out at Thanksgiving, were set nicely, and included small platters of Oreos and tiny cakes, some of which, in fact, sported tiny frosted carrots.

Four places were set at the kitchen table.

"Wh-where's Mr. Fuzzypants?!" My sister stammered, bottom lip beginning to tremble. "I didn't tell anyone! I promise! Did the magic not work?"

"The magic worked, sweetie." He kissed her on the head. "But Mr. Fuzzypants told me he was running late and for us to start tea without him. He'll be here shortly."

"He *said* that? He talked to you?"

Dad nodded. "He did. That's part of the magic."

My sister's mouth dropped open, and she looked like she'd stumbled into an extra Christmas morning. Even I couldn't help being happy to see her so excited.

Taking a deep breath, I still looked for whatever trick Dad was playing, mostly to see if I could help more because I really *did* like seeing Mercedes happy—and I was worried how she'd react if Mr. Fuzzypants *didn't* show up as Dad promised. Dad poured us each a cup of tea.

Mercedes started slurping up her tea right away. I picked up the cup and sniffed, then glanced at Dad, who had poured himself some water.

"No tea for you?" I had to ask.

He shook his head. "Tea has tannins, which make me sick. That's why I can't drink a lot of wines or eat certain foods."

"Oh." I tilted my head from side to side, weighing what he said. I remembered that about Dad, especially when we went to restaurants and he asked a lot of questions. I sipped the tea gingerly, letting it roll across my tongue. "Honey?"

"I figured you'd both prefer sweet," he said.

I pursed my lips. The tea felt like it was sucking some of the spit from the inside of my cheeks. After the honey flavor went away, it tasted almost like dirt or humid summer days. I wasn't sure if I liked it, so I sipped it again, enjoying the honey, in any case.

When I'd mostly finished my first cup of tea, I heard a knock. It made me jump, even though a part of my brain was pretty sure Dad had just knocked on the bottom of the table. It wasn't easy to hear the doors from the kitchen. Aha! This was the trick part. I wanted to pay attention, except another part of my brain *didn't* want to pay attention. It kept seeing things move just out of where I was looking.

Magic? Was I seeing magic?

"That's Mr. Fuzzypants, now!" Dad's voice sounded cheery and made me think of a cartoon character. Not any one in particular, just a cartoon character of Dad, which was weird. He got up from the table and went down the stairs to the side door and the cellar, closing the door behind him.

Definitely some trick that he didn't want us to see.

He came back into the kitchen cradling a blanket-swathed Mr. Fuzzypants.

And Mr. Fuzzypants was moving!

Mercedes squealed with delight.

Dad placed him in the fourth spot at the kitchen table, where Mom used to sit. He put him right on the table next to the empty plate, where he dropped a handful of long grass.

"Oh, Mister Fuzzypants! It's so good to see you!" cooed my sister.

I couldn't take my eyes off the bunny. He stayed in the blanket, but he was definitely moving…wriggling, or something. The dead bunny fixed me with one eye, one eye that seemed to have turned a mahogany brown like Mercedes's or Mom's, and then turned his attention to my sister.

"Oh, I missed you, too. What's it like in Bunny Heaven?" Mercedes asked.

It's not like I'd spent a ton of time around the rabbit, but I knew the noises he made. Mostly he just grunted and thumped his back feet at me; he didn't like me very much. But sometimes, when Mercedes was holding him and stroking his nose, he would make little popping noises.

What I heard was an eerie chirp along with the popping noises, like a high-pitched voice I couldn't quite make out. I froze in my seat, staring.

"Really? All grass everywhere? And rainbows every day?" Mercedes clasped her hands and tilted her head as she kept talking to Mr. Fuzzypants.

"Would you like some cake, Portia?"

I nearly jumped in my seat at Dad's voice. I glanced between him and the sort-of talking dead rabbit on the kitchen table. My heart was hammering. No, I didn't want to eat. I didn't feel very well at all.

What I said was: "Mom wouldn't have liked the rabbit on the table."

Mercedes scowled at me. "How else will he reach his food?"

"He doesn't *need* food. He—"

"Mercedes?" My dad interrupted. "Would you like to hold Mister Fuzzypants?"

"Yes! Yes, please!"

"Ok. I'll bring him to you."

Dad placed the blanket-wrapped bunny in my sister's arms, where it seemed to wiggle and make that eerie chirping even more.

"He's still cold," my sister said.

"That's normal," my dad explained. "He's supposed to be in Bunny Heaven, not in his body. He can't stay with us very long."

Good, I thought. The sooner Mr. Fuzzypants was gone for good, the better. I was also starting to feel really cold.

"But I can feel him moving! Like he's vibrating and stuff! He missed me, Daddy; he says so!"

"I'm sure he does, but he belongs in Bunny Heaven. He just came down to give you one last goodbye since he didn't get to last week."

"No! It's not his last goodbye! Why can't he come for tea again?"

The muscles in Dad's face tensed up. He was squatting beside my sister, who was petting the not-quite-dead Mr. Fuzzypants. "Because it takes a lot of work for him to come back down from Bunny Heaven—"

"But he says he wants to! You can hear him now, right? You said you could hear him."

"Sweetheart, it's not fair to take him out of Bunny Heaven—"

"But he loves me, Daddy!"

I couldn't stop staring at Mr. Fuzzypants. His eyes had grown more red, and not a nice warm red. More like "something's wrong alarm" red. I didn't like how he was looking at my sister. Or worse, my dad. There was something very wrong, and I could feel it like bad food in my stomach. If Dad really *had* done magic, maybe he'd made a mistake? Everyone makes mistakes. What if Mr. Fuzzypants had come back wrong, like a zombie or…evil?

Then, he looked right at me, and it felt like I was getting sucked out of the whole world!

From far away, I heard Dad say something about Mr. Fuzzypants having to get back to Bunny Heaven for an important meeting or something, and then he "helped" Mr. Fuzzypants back to the side door.

Once I couldn't see the evil rabbit any more, I snapped back into the world. Everything was louder and brighter, and I felt very, very tired.

Mercedes was crying into her empty tea cup about wanting to go visit Bunny Heaven.

As for me, I was convinced the Mr. Fuzzypants who had joined us for tea had *nothing* to do with Bunny Heaven—or any Heaven for that matter.

I **felt sick for the rest of the day, but I remember hearing** Mercedes refuse to go to bed until Dad agreed that Mr. Fuzzypants could come back for tea another time. That made me feel even sicker.

I wanted to throw a tantrum like Mercedes would. I was *this close*. But I felt too tired and sick.

That night, I had a nightmare about Mr. Fuzzypants chasing me around in a really big outdoor bunny pen. He had glowing red eyes and grass was growing from my arms and he was going to eat it!

I don't think I slept much at all the rest of Wednesday, and that made me a different kind of sick on Thursday.

"I'm too sick to go to school," I told Dad when he knocked on my door.

When he came in, I expected him to be suspicious. It's not like I'd never tried to get out of school before. He wasn't, though. In fact, he looked kind of nervous as he came over to the bed and sat beside me, brushing my hair out of my face. "What's wrong, sweetheart?"

"I just feel sick."

"Sick like how?"

"Just sick. In my tummy. And I didn't sleep well last night."

He sat there thinking, then said, "You know if you stay home, Mercedes will want to stay home, too."

"I don't care. I don't feel good." I wrapped my blankets around me.

"All right. You can stay home today, Portia. Let me try to get Mercedes to go to school."

He couldn't, of course, and Mercedes pitched another fit. I dozed a few times, but more nightmares crept in. This time it was an evil, red-eyed Mercedes chasing me around a bunny pen trying to eat me. All of me.

I woke up more scared than I'd been after the other dream, with my stomach even more sick. Stupid dreams. I never told anyone, because I was the mature one, but I really was scared of my sister when she threw her tantrums. She was bigger than me, and she's *really* strong when she throws or hits. I'd seen Dad, Mom, and Miss Carrie have to restrain her during really bad tantrums, and they had a hard time doing that. She'd given Mom a black eye once, and I'd wanted to hit her back, but Mom had said I couldn't.

"Mercedes doesn't always understand what she's doing or how strong she is," Mom had said. "And she doesn't understand why you'd hit her."

"Sometimes she does!" I had argued. "Sometimes Mercedes definitely hits on purpose!"

Mom had sighed. I remembered that the black eye had made her almost not look like Mom, like I'd been looking at a funhouse mirror reflection that I didn't quite recognize. "Listen to me, sweetie. I know it's hard for you to understand, too, but promise me this, okay? If Mercedes ever has a tantrum around you, if she ever tries to hurt you—even if you're not sure—go find an adult for help. Promise me that, Luxury Car Two?"

Of course I'd promised. Remembering that didn't help me being sick. Worse, it made me want to cry more. I rolled even tighter into my blankets until they were like a cocoon around me. It was a little too warm, but I didn't care. I felt safer from the evil zombie bunnies and my scary sister.

***I** don't want Mr. Fuzzypants to come to tea again,"* I told my Dad before Mercedes joined us for breakfast and after another answering machine message from Mr. Murray. "I think the magic is what made me sick."

Dad looked at me wearing a face that made me think of when I'd done something wrong and I was trying not to get caught. He took a deep breath. "I'm sorry, sweetie. I...I promised Misty we'd do it again, but I'll be more careful this time. It shouldn't make you sick—and this will be the *last* time, I promise."

I frowned. I wanted to tell him that I thought Mr. Fuzzypants was evil and going to hurt us. But then Mercedes bounced in, and Dad's focus was on making her eat all her eggs and reminding her, *very strongly*, that she couldn't tell anyone about Wednesday's tea party.

She made the zipped and locked lips signs again, and I slouched in my seat. I wanted to shove my food away, but since I'd hardly eaten yesterday, I was too hungry, so I decided to balance inhaling breakfast with serious sulking.

***F** or the next tea party, Mr. Fuzzypants really did have* red eyes. The tea tasted a little different, less like dirt and summer and more like honey.

I drank my whole cup this time because I needed to think about something besides my sister's conversation with her evil back-from-the-dead pet. Watching her snuggle Mr. Fuzzypants in her arms like he was alive made me sick again.

He still didn't *do* much, and it seemed like he couldn't move very easily in his undead state, but he *looked* at me. And I could hear his wicked chitter-popping language that only Mercedes and Dad seemed to understand. That flipped my stomach like the roller-coaster Dad once snuck me onto while Mercedes was having Mom time. Only now, I could actually admit I was terrified.

Except the look in Mr. Fuzzypants's eyes said he might hurt someone if I said what I was feeling.

I didn't want him to hurt anyone, not even my annoying special needs sister who wanted her dead bunny back.

I didn't know what to do.

*I*made myself go to school the next day, even though I'd had even worse nightmares than last time. If I stayed home, Mercedes would stay home and I'd lose out on my Dad time after school yet again. And I hadn't had *any* Dad time since the stupid bunny died and came back to life.

I *hated* Mr. Fuzzypants.

And he probably knew it, too, which was why he was making me feel scared of him.

I decided that in my Dad time after school I'd tell him. It was *his* magic that had done this, so he should be able to control Mr. Fuzzypants and send him back to wherever he was *really* from. That was probably why the evil zombie bunny hadn't wanted me to say anything to Dad! He knew Dad had the power to make sure he never came back. I'd tell Dad and everything would be back to normal.

*N*othing was going to be back to normal, and Dad wouldn't keep his promises *to me*!

Mercedes threw a fit right when she got back home from school about wanting tea with Mr. Fuzzypants again because this was *her time* to play with him. And that was the last straw for me, so I threw a tantrum.

I got grounded, because I knew better. Mercedes got Dad time. It was so unfair!

The worst part of it all was, by the weekend, Dad had lost two more days of work, probably more sleep than I had with my nightmares, and we were going to have tea with Mr. Fuzzypants again next week.

I never hated my sister so much.

But when I went to bed, the thought came to me that this was all Mr. Fuzzypants's fault. He wanted my sister all to himself, so he was making me hate her and making Dad mad at me so he wouldn't listen and send him back to evil zombie bunny Hell.

I had to do something.

*W*hen the next tea party rolled around, I had a plan. Mr. Fuzzypants probably didn't realize it, but getting me angry enough to make Dad ground me was what made it work.

Mercedes was "sick," or so she said, and she'd begged to stay home. She'd woken up screaming a few nights this week too, even after Daddy had promised this stupid tea party. I had a feeling Mr. Fuzzypants was doing something awful, and the part of her mind that worked all right—because sometimes she really could be smart about things—was trying to warn her with nightmares. I needed to work fast.

As I walked in the door, I headed right to my room.

Mercedes stopped me. "Portia, aren't you coming to tea?"

"I'm grounded," I said. "I can't come to tea."

Dad peeked around the corner with that guilty, sad look on his face. "You can join us, Portia. I know this has been a hard week for you, and I'm sorry for that."

Well, crud. There went my plan, just like that. I could say "I don't want to" and start another big fight and probably make Mercedes have another fit…or I could just settle down for tea.

I glanced at the kitchen table. In the empty spot that used to be Mom's, I thought I could see Mr. Fuzzypants's evil red eyes laughing at me.

I wouldn't let him win!

"I…I think the tannins in the tea are what are making me sick, like they do for you, Dad. I didn't want to make you worry last week, but I was sick, and that was why I acted up. May I please be excused?" I looked at Mercedes. "You can have Dad and Mr. Fuzzypants all to yourself this time."

Mercedes's lips twitched. "But I like having tea with you, too. You're my favorite sister."

A warm feeling spread across my chest hearing her say that. I was her *only* sister, but I knew what she meant.

Dad put a hand on my head. "But you don't want your favorite sister sick, do you, Misty?"

My sister thought a moment and shook her head. She leaned over and gave me a kiss on the cheek. "We can save her some cake and cookies, right?"

Dad nodded and placed one of the tiny squares of chocolate cake and two of the Soft Batch chocolate chip cookies—things he knew were my favorites—on a plate for me. "Wait in your room, then. After tea, we can have some time together, just you and me, okay?"

I nodded and continued up to my room. Phew! Portia 1, Mr. Fuzzypants 0. Time for round two!

I watched my clock for a count of twenty-one minutes. People are absolutely right that clocks move way slower when you're watching them. But I wanted to be exact, and 21 was a lucky number. I'd played 21 plenty of times with Dad during our time when it was too snowy or cold to play outside.

Once the time passed, I put on my super-soft ducky slippers that made no noise ever and crept down the stairs. Dad would have already done whatever magic by now, and I wouldn't be part of it, so I might see something I could do. Maybe I could show them all that Mr. Fuzzypants was evil if I wasn't affected by the magic.

Sneak, sneak, sneak, I headed toward the kitchen. The stove and wall at the kitchen doorway made kind of a hallway where, if I crouched low enough, I could hide. I'd gotten pretty good at surprising Mom and Dad a few times from this set-up.

The phone rang; I froze. Mercedes began to whine about it interrupting tea, and Dad told her to just ignore it. I don't know what it is about ringing phones, but the sound made me tense my shoulders up and feel like I was holding my breath. I wondered if it was some counterplan by Mr. Fuzzypants...

"Hey, Hank, it's me again, Don..." Mr. Murray again, and he was talking fast and almost as whiney as Mercedes. "Look, I *really* need that Mustang. How about I just stop by tomorrow and grab it? I, uh, know where Tina kept the keys and everything; it'll be no problem at all." I swallowed hard, hearing him say Mom's name... "I'll even bring by, you know, whatever she was promised to get for it later in the week. And fix that leaky freezer before summer comes and you gotta worry about mold..."

My chest hurt like I couldn't breathe, and then I blew out all the air that I'd been holding in my lungs. It might've been the strangeness in Mr. Murray's voice that brought the sickness back to my stomach, but it felt like something more. Mom and I had been working on the Mustang together. And she was going to teach me how to fix the freezer. I remembered her saying "before it gets warm and we need to worry about mold" and complaining about cleaning up downstairs. I know Dad couldn't fix stuff like Mom could, but it *wasn't* Mr. Murray's job...and it *wasn't* his Mustang!

Mercedes seemed to have a similar reaction, because she'd started a low keening as soon as Mr. Murray started to talk, as if she'd forgotten all about her stupid tea and zombie bunny.

Okay, maybe Mr. Murray wasn't so annoying if somehow him calling during the tea broke the bad magic.

Dad started talking. I didn't dare look up from my hiding spot, but I pictured him hugging Mercedes and rocking her. "No one's taking Mom's and Uncle James's Mustang away, baby. Don't worry. Listen, even Mr. Fuzzypants doesn't like Mr. Murray." Dad gasped. "Mr. Fuzzypants, you shouldn't say that word! Do I need to wash your mouth out with soap?"

Mercedes started giggling, and their weird conversations started back up. *Really, Dad?* I thought. Well, I would show him that Mr. Fuzzypants was evil and had to go and never come back.

Staying low, I crept a little closer. Everyone seemed distracted again with Mercedes asking, "What does the grass taste like? Are there any people there? Did you see Mom?"

The last question sent ice into my lungs. Mr. Fuzzypants was evil now, so no way he'd have seen Mom anywhere!

But he apparently said something otherwise because my sister responded, "Does she say she misses me and Portia and Daddy?"

It took all of my will to not scream that Mom was in Real Heaven. I had to be strong. I had to prove how bad Mr. Fuzzypants was so Dad could use his magic to send him away forever!

Finally able to take another deep breath, I peeked around the stove to get a better look. Dad had come around the table and was handing Mercedes Mr. Fuzzypants to cuddle. The rabbit looked…different.

He wasn't wiggling, first of all. He was hard and stiff in the blanket. I could see the pinkish skin beneath the fur on his face. His eyes were that same glassy *dead* I saw in our yard the day he died. Not red. Not looking at me.

Dad and Mercedes had their backs to me, so I crept out a little further to get a better look. Mercedes put Mr. Fuzzypants on her shoulder, and he still looked dead. She cooed and stroked him. More white fur from his face stuck to her fingers.

What kind of trick was this? How was he hiding from me? What was I missing?

Focusing on the dead bunny eyes, I took another step out from around the stove.

And promptly tripped on the ducky head of my slipper. I smacked my head on the corner of the stove and yelped in pain. The pot of steaming water on the stove must've got jostled and a small splash hit my fingers where I grabbed on to catch myself.

I couldn't keep from yowling again from the burning water.

Mercedes shrieked, dropping Mr. Fuzzypants, who landed on the floor with a heavy *thunk*. Seeing him lying there, she started screaming.

"Mr. Fuzzypants! Mr. Fuzzypants! You scared him away! You hurt him!"

"He's dead!" I yelled back, feeling hot tears run down my cheeks. I alternated between shaking my scalded hand and rubbing my temple where I'd cracked it on the stove. "And he's not anywhere near Mom! Mom's in Heaven. It's all a lie!"

"Don't say that!" Mercedes yelled back. "It's not a lie! You're a bad sister to say that to me!" Her eyes got really angry, and she started coming toward me.

Dad reached out and grabbed Mercedes's arms. "Portia, go to your room now."

"No!" I shouted. "No! It's not fair! I didn't do anything wrong. Mr. Fuzzypants is trying to hurt people, and I'm just trying to help!"

"Mr. Fuzzypants wouldn't hurt anyone! You're an awful, awful liar!" Mercedes lunged at me again, and Dad pulled her arms into a lock.

He glared at me. "Portia! Bed! Now!" Sweat dripped off his brow as he adjusted his hold on my sister, who was trying to flail her arms and stomp. Her face was red, and her lips and eyes twisted so they looked almost like a demon.

I ran to my room and slammed my door shut. I shoved a bunch of my clothes under the crack to wedge it closed, then I threw myself on my bed and cried.

It was all Mr. Fuzzypants's fault! He was turning my sister evil. I'd bet he'd been the one to trip me so I couldn't sneak up and find some way to stop the magic.

It wasn't fair!

I hugged my pillows tightly and cried and screamed and cried and screamed.

I **must've fallen asleep like that, because I don't remember** anything else. When I woke up, it was a few minutes before my alarm would go off anyway.

Slowly, I realized I was in my jammies and tucked in. I saw the piles of clothes from under my door angled inward. Dad must've wiggled his way in.

At least Mr. Fuzzypants hadn't succeeded in making Dad hate me yet.

I got up, rubbing the crusties from my eyes and reaching for a tissue to blow my nose. A glob of blood came out with the snot.

I whimpered and tried to wipe and blow again, but more blood came out.

Damn Mr. Fuzzypants! He was doing this to me too!

He didn't realize I was mature for my age and had had nosebleeds before. I made myself be calm and carefully held more tissues my nose until it stopped bleeding. According to my clock, it took almost five minutes.

I still felt woozy from crying, so it took even longer to brush my teeth and get dressed for school. By the time I got downstairs, Mercedes was already in her spot, eating.

She looked like she'd cried all night too. Her eyes were ringed with red, and her nose was red, and her whole face was puffy. She glared at me as I sat down.

Dad, who looked even worse with dark circles under his swollen eyes, shuffled over and kissed me on the top of my head. "I was just going to come and get you, Portia. How are you this morning?"

I scowled at him.

He frowned, but before he could scold me for being rude, Mercedes piped up. "Dad is going to have another tea party for Mr. Fuzzypants today, and you aren't going to ruin this one!"

He gave her a look now. "And this *will* be the last one, Mercedes. Portia is right. Mr. Fuzzypants doesn't belong here. And we're not being fair to Portia. She and I used to have our dates, every Wednesday and Thursday afternoon. We haven't had that since that first tea party, so that is why she's been so angry and hurt. You will say goodbye to Mr. Fuzzypants this afternoon, and that's it. Do you understand?"

Mercedes screwed her face up and started to whine.

"Do you like making your little sister cry like you did yesterday? Do you mean to hurt her feelings?" Now Dad's eyes were scolding Mercedes. My heart was beating warmer in my chest. Mr. Fuzzypants didn't have any power over Dad! He was right to be scared of Dad sending him away forever. Dad must be seeing through his evil plans, so everything would be all right!

Mercedes relaxed a little and looked at me. She was still glaring, but not as hard, and she shook her head. She didn't *want* to hurt me.

"Good," Dad said, and with that, he hustled us off to school.

I was more bouncy than Mercedes as we walked up to the house. We didn't talk, but she wasn't sulking. She seemed…thoughtful.

I didn't care. I was glad Mr. Fuzzypants was finally going away for good! Once he was gone, he couldn't make her have so many tantrums. Dad could go back to work, and most everything would go back to normal.

Well, as normal as it had been since Mom died.

Thoughts about Mom kept creeping in. Maybe next time Dad and I had our time, we could just sit in the Mustang and play 21, even if it was really nice outside. I liked that idea; I'd tell him about it tomorrow.

"Da-ad, we're ho-ome!" I called as we came through the front door.

We headed directly to the kitchen. A pot of water was half-empty, boiling on the stove. I, very carefully, reached over and turned off the burner. On the counter was the honey and a plastic bag of what looked like leaves and dirt. That must be the tea.

But no Dad.

"Daaaady?" Mercedes called, sitting down in her spot at the table. "Are we going to have our goodbye tea now?"

I looked around the kitchen. The door that led to the side foyer and cellar was ajar and moving in a breeze. I pushed it wider and noticed the side door was also open. The rug was damp. There were some water smears on the top step.

"Dad?" I called. My heart felt like it was going to pound through my chest. There was no answer.

"We're not supposed to go down cellar without Mom or Dad," Mercedes told me from where she sat at the table, ready for tea. I could hear a waver in her voice. She must have had the funny, fluttery feeling I did in my lungs and throat. Breathing felt funny, like it was work.

"I-I think Dad's downstairs," I said. "I'm going to go check. You stay here. That way, if I'm wrong, I'm the only one who will get in trouble."

"Okay." Her voice sounded unsure.

On a whim, while she wasn't looking, I grabbed my softball bat from behind the open side door where I'd left it. Then, I crept down the stairs.

"Dad?" I couldn't make my voice go any louder. What if he just couldn't hear me? Maybe he had to fix something on his workbench before tea and got distracted?

What if Mr. Fuzzypants had done something so Dad couldn't use his magic to send him back forever?

There are exactly twelve stairs from the side door landing to the cellar. I know; I've counted them a bunch of times. It felt like way more as I went one step at a time. I stayed close to the sides, where they creaked less. I don't know why, but I felt I had to sneak.

At the bottom of the cellar, there are two rooms. One has Mom's and Dad's workbenches and tools, as well as the lock room for Dad's hunting guns and the dangerous tools. The other has the laundry machines and the big freezer.

I turned on the light and looked at the floor. Wet partial shoe-prints led to the workbench room. I followed them. Mom's main car toolbox was missing, but that was it. Had Mr. Murray come anyway? There was only one set of footprints going to the workbench and back to where I stood by the stairs. I vaguely remembered, as we'd walked into the house, noticing Dad's car was parked out front, like when Mom would work on cars and need to get in and out of the driveway easily.

Had Dad lied about that, too? Would he really have given the Mustang back to Mr. Murray? I know it was really Uncle James's, not Mom's, but still! I was about to go back up when I heard the pump for the freezer kick on. It sounded louder than usual. Probably because I was scared, I told myself. But I turned on the light to the laundry-freezer room anyway.

I couldn't make out what I was seeing before I dropped my aluminum softball bat and screamed, "Dad!"

My brain pieced the picture together.

Dad lay on the ground, blood on his forehead, eyes closed. There was a puddle on the floor with a slip mark—but no footprints. There was blood on the top corner of the freezer.

The freezer cover was propped open by Mr. Fuzzypants's body. His glassy eyes stared at nothing.

I screamed again, this time unable to make words.

From what sounded like far away, I heard stomping and stumbling, a few yelps, and even a word I knew my sister and I weren't supposed to use—in my sister's voice. Then she was beside me.

"Daddy! Daddy! Daddy!" Mercedes's voice sounded both louder and more slurred than usual.

She ran to him and tried to sit him up. She pulled him until he leaned on the freezer. His head lolled to the side like he was napping.

"Daddy! Daddy!" she continued to wail.

All of a sudden, my mind started to work. "His phone! See if he has his phone! We have to call 911!"

"NO!" Mercedes screamed.

"What do you mean, 'no'?!" I rushed over to Dad and started rooting in his pockets. His body was still loose, not hard, not like Mr. Fuzzypants when Mercedes found him. He could just be hurt. There wasn't a lot of blood. Not really.

"I said NO!" Mercedes shoved me away.

She *was* really strong. It had been a long time since she lashed out at me. Mom and Dad were always good at stopping that. I flew backward, slipping on the water and landing on my butt. I skidded, slamming the back of my head on the flat side of the washing machine.

The pain from my butt and head made me see stars. I fought through them and tried to make a calm voice, like Mom or Dad would have made. "Misty, we have to call 911. Dad could be really hurt and they can help him."

"No! If we call 911, I'll go to jail. I'm eighteen, and I'll go to jail!"

"Wait, what?" Stars and pain aside, I focused on her.

"911 is the police, and Mr. Murray said I'd go to jail if I ever called the police, ever. He said I was eighteen, and because I was eighteen I'd go to jail and they might fry me in an electric chair!"

"What?" I shook my head. I don't think this would have made sense even if I wasn't possibly concussed. "What? When did Mr. Murray say that? Is he here now?"

"No! I don't want him here. But when Mom fell down the stairs. That's what he told me. He made me go back to bed, and he said she'd be fine in the morning, but she wasn't. I don't want to go to jail, Portia! I don't want to fry in an electric chair!"

I had no words. Not for several seconds. What was Mr. Murray doing at our house when Mom fell? Dad had found Mom when he came home from work. He had called me at 5AM and told Jennie's mom to bring me home. It had been my first sleepover, ever.

What had my sister seen?

Mercedes filled up the space of my silence. "I know what will help!"

She ran upstairs. Still rubbing my head, I tried to stand. I felt dizzy, and it felt like I'd landed on the sharp end of a knife. I made it to my feet, but I could hardly walk. Inching my way over to Dad, I had to walk by Mr. Fuzzypants's body. Cold air from the freezer shivered goosebumps up my arms. Even though his dead eyes weren't red and glowing, they still seemed to be looking at me. Careful of the massive puddle that extended far beyond the pile of towels under one corner of the freezer, I launched myself close to Dad.

He wasn't warm, and he smelled. That was bad, I knew. I went for his left pocket where he kept his cell phone and called 911.

"911, what's your emergency?"

"My name is Portia Cartwright, and I live at 17 Schick Avenue in Holyfield, Massachusetts... My dad fell and he's not moving and my sister is very scared. She's got special needs, so she doesn't have control over herself, and she might hurt someone if she knew I was calling, so please send help, but tell them no sirens or anything or it will scare her and I'm not big enough to hold her. Please hurry."

I heard Misty's feet back on the stairs going slow and careful, so I ended the call and shoved the phone back in Dad's pocket. I put my fingers on his neck, where the gym coaches have us check for our pulse and heart rate. I didn't feel anything.

"Please, please, be okay, Dad. Please..." I whispered.

Mercedes was holding the teapot in her arms and clutching two of the teacups. "We can bring him back, like Mr. Fuzzypants. It's soon enough to make it work!"

"What are you talking about?" I asked my sister.

"It's soon! If—if Dad's gone, we can bring him back for good, I think. I asked, yesterday, why we couldn't have Mom for tea, and he said it was because he learned the magic too late for it to work. And Mr. Fuzzypants could only come back for a little bit at a time because it had been a week after he died. If we do this right now, Dad will come back and be okay!" Her hands were shaking as she gripped the teapot with the potholder and poured two splattery cups of tea.

"Mercedes, I don't think—"

"Drink it!" she shouted at me. "If you don't, it'll be your fault if Dad doesn't come back!"

I cowered as close to Dad as I could, but Mercedes looked like she really might hurt me. I grabbed the cup from the floor. Even though it burned a lot, I drank it all down. Every disgusting drop.

Then, I started to gag. It tasted way more of dirt than honey this time. In my head, I pieced together my sister's logic that more tea would make whatever magic there was stronger, and it needed to be stronger to bring back something big and human.

I gripped Dad's shoulder, which felt cold and gross, with one hand while I clutched my stomach with the other.

I was going to puke!

I looked at my sister, who was talking to Dad, telling him to come back. She carefully took Mr. Fuzzypants from where the freezer door had trapped him. He started to wriggle in her arms, and his eyes turned red again. He'd won! He'd gotten rid of Dad so Dad couldn't send him back, and now my sister was all his!

My stomach heaved and I gasped, knocking Dad back down.

"Be careful, Portia! Don't hurt Dad!"

I looked at my sister. Her eyes were red like Mr. Fuzzypants's eyes. I took one big step over Dad's chest and tried to move away from her.

She put Mr. Fuzzypants in Dad's lap and reached over. "Help me sit him back up, Portia!"

"No! No! This is all wrong. This isn't going to work, Misty! We need real help… I'm…I'm going to…"

I puked all over the cellar floor. The nasty tea burned even worse on the way back up.

"Portia! What's wrong?"

"I-I-I…" Like a flock of birds were all trapped in my chest, I felt a million beating wings stopping my breath and beating in my still-sick stomach. Everything was wrong. Everything. Evil Mr. Fuzzypants was on top of Dad now. I couldn't see clearly. There were too many tears in my eyes, and they burned too. In my head, I could hear Mr. Fuzzypants laughing.

Then, I heard something else. The crank of an engine. I knew that cranking sound. I'd sat in the car for it. Mom would even have me, her "best assistant," push on the gas when she needed to check stuff.

The car!

Maybe the magic tea had done something right. Maybe Mom was here and it was her footprints and that's why her toolbox was missing! Mom would make it all better.

I ran out of the freezer room and up the stairs. I slipped once, banging my knee hard. It hurt, and I knew in my head it hurt, but the pain didn't stop me from running out of the cellar and outside. In my tummy, the furious and terrified birds seemed to stop beating me sick for a minute and helped push me out.

The Mustang engine turned over again and held its rumble.

The garage door was open, so I ran in, ready to see Mom. She'd drive me away from Mr. Fuzzypants before he could do something awful to me too.

Only when I got to the driver side door, it was Mr. Murray behind the steering wheel. I stopped and stared at him.

He stared back at me, his bright blue eyes looking even more scary than Mr. Fuzzypants's red eyes.

Mr. Murray opened the driver's door and started to get out. I backed away—further into the garage was the only place to go. Something about him terrified me worse than zombie Mr. Fuzzypants. "Portia, honey, what's going on?"

Something in his voice rollercoastered my stomach and all the scared birds inside me. "You can't have Uncle James's and Mom's car!" I screamed, and then doubled over and threw up all over Mr. Murray.

"What the…" He shook his arms and flicked my dirt-honey-tea puke from his shirt and jeans, mouth gaping as he stared at himself.

That bought me a second. Mr. Murray and the car door blocked my way directly out, so I ran around the tail, hoping I could run faster than the skinny, wild-eyed man could chase me. But Mr. Murray dove back into the car and shoved the passenger door wide open, blocking my way. I threw myself to the ground, trying to slide like I was stealing a base, but the rubberized floor didn't let me get far, and the motion sent another spike up my spine and another into my knee. I rolled over and did my best to crawl, painfully, under the door and toward the open garage front.

That took too long. I heard the driver's door slam and Mr. Murray's feet run over. I was halfway under the door. He reached for me. I rolled under the car, feeling his hand just miss my arm. The floor below me was cold, but hot air rumbled from the engine above.

Mr. Murray was there when Mom fell down the stairs. He told Mercedes not to call the police. Strangely, after puking, my mind seemed to be working better. I knew Mr. Murray was going to hurt me if I let him. I couldn't let him.

He slammed the passenger-side door.

"Portia, why don't you just come out from under there? I'm not going to hurt you."

Like I was going to believe that. Especially after what Mercedes said about him having been in the house when Mom fell down the stairs. I didn't even answer him.

"I called your dad yesterday and we worked this all out. I don't know why you're acting like this."

I couldn't even think of any words to say. Had he…had he done something to Dad too? I watched his feet walk to the front of the garage, and I heard the click and hum of the big door coming down. For a second, I debated crawling and making a dash for it before it closed, but I could see his brown work boots right in front of the car. Then, I saw him walk to the back of the garage. I heard a scrape of something big getting pulled off of Mom's shelves in the back. He clomped back to the front of the car like he was carrying something.

I saw the red flash of a gas container as liquid splashed just next to me.

"Do you smell that, Portia? You know what gas smells like, right?"

I did, but I wasn't going to answer. I edged away as the gas started dripping toward me. There wasn't much, but still... Twisting my neck, I glanced up at the underside of the car that was getting hotter. I knew it was dangerous to spill gas near a running car. All the gas stations had signs that said so.

Mr. Murray walked to the passenger side of the car, where the side door to the garage was. He splashed more gas. A few drops even reached me despite my trying to move away.

"I know you're a smart girl, Portia. You used to help your mommy work on the cars, right?"

I still wasn't going to answer.

"You know that gas is very, very flammable, right?"

Yes, I did. And Mom always had me be careful around the gas canister. But...she also sat with me when we watched all the *MythBusters* shows about cars. Mr. Murray wasn't splashing a *lot* of gas, and I knew it usually took more than a few drips to really start a fire... And though he'd scared Mercedes, he hadn't *hurt* her. He could have just been trying to scare me.

But who wants to take the chance of getting burned alive? But the thought of facing him, with his monster-bright eyes and...and... something else I couldn't put my finger on. *That* something scared me more than the splashes of gas and kept me where I was. For the moment.

He walked to the back of the car and splashed more gasoline. Then, he came back to the driver's side. If I edged away more, I'd be squirming through the lines of gasoline. He splashed again. The nozzle was *this close* to my face. I tried to roll away, but now it was on my shirt and my pants. Not a lot, but I could smell it.

I couldn't help but gag. I remembered…gas *fumes* were what burned. I squeezed as flat as I could, wondering if something from under the running car would be enough to catch me on fire.

Mr. Murray walked over to the side door of the garage.

"Portia, I have a lighter with me. You've seen in the movies what happens if I light it and throw it in these puddles, right?"

I pressed my lips together, even though I was shivering without the cold. *MythBusters* had also been specific about how *that* Hollywood trick was impossible without a Zippo lighter. Still, the feeling of birds on a rollercoaster thumped all over my entire body now. Muscles jerked and tugged like they wanted to break out of my skin.

"I'm going to count to five, Portia. If you're not out of there by the time I hit five, I'm going to light my lighter and run out this door, and you'll be on fire before you can get out from under there. And you'll be burned alive. And it's going to hurt an awful lot. Do you understand me?"

I held my breath. Now what?

"Now, I just want to talk to you, Portia. Just come out, and we'll talk. Or, I can light this garage, and you, on fire. Which would you prefer?"

I swallowed hard. Every part of me shook, and my tears burned like they were on fire already.

"One… Two… Three…" I heard a metal clink. It *did* sound like a Zippo! I know; Mom had one because sometimes she smoked clove cigarettes. Mr. Murray took a deep breath. "Fo—"

"I'm coming out! I'm coming out!" I rolled and squirmed toward the driver's side, the farthest away from him that I could be. More stinky gas wet my clothes and even my hair. Maybe, if I could get him away from the side door…

"That's a good girl."

I was too scared to scowl at him. I was not his good girl!

"Now, come over here."

I glared at him through the car window. He held up the shiny metal lighter and flicked its top open and closed. Almost definitely a Zippo.

"I'm still closer to the door than you are. And you won't get the big door to come up in time to get out. You're covered in gas."

I gritted my teeth, then headed around the front of the car. The doorbell button for the automatic opener was right there. He was only a few feet away. He'd have been really dumb if he locked the side door. He wouldn't light things on fire if he didn't have an easy way out.

I smacked my hand on the door opener.

"You little bitch!" He lunged at me. I lunged back, like I wanted to tackle him in football. I almost took him down because he wasn't expecting it. I got by him and grabbed the side door. My hands were just twisting the doorknob when a tearing pain yanked at my scalp.

I screamed, cursing the ponytail he'd grabbed. Next hair cut would be short, like a boy's!

I didn't scream much before he shoved a part of his fist in my mouth.

I bit, tasting sweat and blood. I kicked. I punched anywhere I could reach.

But Mr. Murray was even bigger than Dad. And though he looked skinny, he was way strong. Even when I felt, for sure, that my sneaker heel hit him in the shin not once, but twice, all he did was grunt.

He flipped open the trunk and threw me in, then swung one leg over the bumper and leaned his knee on my stomach. I gagged on the half-a-hand that was in my mouth and tried to bite harder. I could taste blood, but that only made me gag even more.

Between bites, he yanked his hand free and slapped me across the face. Before I could scream for help, his whole clammy hand was over my mouth and nose, cupped so my teeth couldn't reach him. I tossed my head, trying to break free. I tried to scream anyway, but I knew it didn't get far, not even with the big garage door open now.

Besides, a part of me remembered all our closest neighbors worked *normal* hours, and they didn't have kids. No one was home to either side of us, or across the street. Not for at least another hour or two. Even if they were, I wasn't sure they'd even help. The most I saw of them was when they were complaining about the cars in our driveway or looking at us out of the corners of their eyes and talking to each other. Kids notice that sort of thing.

On the other hand, if one of them *was* home, they were probably calling the police; it wouldn't be the first time for that, either. For once, that'd be a good thing.

"Stop this shit right now, Portia." I hated the sound of Mr. Murray's voice. It was both very calm and very angry. I looked up at his eyes. They were really, really bloodshot, which made the blue almost glow. And they seemed to flick randomly at one thing or another every so often. All of the bones in his face looked like they were going to poke right through his skin, and sweat was dripping off of him and onto me. Gross! His voice seemed extra high and extra stammery, like he couldn't quite control his words. "I-I just said I wanted to talk, all right? If you can keep a s-secret, then no one else has to get hurt, okay? Can you keep a secret for me?"

I nodded and stopped struggling. I needed time. What secret would he ask me to keep? Would it be a secret like he'd made Mercedes keep that made her afraid to call the police? Would we be accomplices? That's why my uncle got put in jail—I looked it up on the internet after Dad said Uncle James had taught him the magic. The news said he was charged as an accomplice to a murder. After I'd read up on it, I'd remembered Dad and Mom had said the *real* bad guy was some drug dealer who Uncle James had thought was his friend but hadn't been caught.

I needed time to make some sort of plan, so I nodded, agreeing to his "secret."

"That's-that's a good girl. Now, I'm going to take my hand off of your mouth. If you scream, the deal's off, got it?" Though he sort of looked more relaxed, he still seemed twitchy and…wrong.

I nodded again.

He let go of my face. I didn't scream. I had to think.

But my head was feeling fuzzy again. Possibly from how hard he'd slapped me. The back of my head, where it'd hit the washing machine, was throbbing. The pain in my butt and knee also started to edge back into my brain. Especially my butt, which felt like I was lying on a lot of broken glass. Mr. Murray leaning on me to hold me down wasn't helping, for sure.

And the trunk smelled funky. Kinda like the tea the way Mercedes had made it, only worse.

"Now, Portia. I don't…I don't *want* to kill you, but I'm going to have to hurt you. I'm going to hit you in the back of the head, and it's going to be like you just went to sleep. When you wake up, you're going to say you don't remember who stole your Uncle James's old car, okay? You're never going to say anything about seeing me here, or else I will kill you, and I will send your sister to jail, all by herself with no one to look out for her. Do you understand?"

Maybe he had been bluffing with the gasoline. If he really wanted the car, wouldn't that have burnt up, too?

I sucked in snot and blood from my nose and swallowed it. It burned the back of my throat, and I started coughing. I turned my head to the side to try and spit it all out, along with more puke that was making its way out thanks to Mr. Murray's stupid knee. That's when I saw the boxes full of baggies. All sorts of baggies. A lot had white stuff, some had green leaves, and some had…dried mushrooms?

"I said, 'Do you understand?'" Mr. Murray leaned harder on me, which made me actually gag from the pain. Then he started to ramble; his voice was calm, even though everything about him said he was nervous and tense. He made me think of the chatty homeless people I sometimes saw downtown when Mom left me locked in the car while she ran in somewhere for parts. "I don't want to hurt you, not a kid. I wasn't really going to burn you; I just needed you to come out so we could talk, you know? Figure this all out. I'm sure you're a good kid that wants to do the right thing. I do too. Want to do the right thing. I definitely don't want to kill you. I'm sorry about your mom; I really am. It was an accident. I just need this car is all."

"What about my dad?" I asked. I don't know why; that was how my brain was working. Had he smashed Dad's head on the freezer? He'd known it was leaking...

"What about your dad?" Mr. Murray narrowed his eyes and looked confused. Before he could say anymore, his cell phone rang. He clamped his hand back over my mouth. I tried to squirm, but he leaned harder with his knee. I thought he might break my ribs!

"Yeah, I've got the car and the stuff. It's right here. I'm lookin' at it..." He looked at me with his bloodshot, almost-glowing blue eyes and frowned. "Not really... I mean, it's just the kid." He frowned even more and his already-wide eyes got even wider. "She's just a kid. She'll—" He closed his eyes and scrunched his face. "She's *just a kid.*"

I didn't like where this was going at all.

"...and you don't think..." He looked at me again. "...*that* will draw even more attention?"

I stopped all my struggling and let all sorts of tears go down my face. He didn't want to kill me. I had to believe that, and if I looked like just some cute, good little girl, maybe he wouldn't be able to.

He closed his eyes again, making a face at his phone. I could hear the other person yelling, but not what he was saying. I made a little whimper. *Look at me. I'm just a kid. A really nice kid most of the time.*

"Right, right, I got it. I...I understand. I get it. Fine!" His voice grew angrier and colder with every word he said.

I whimpered louder. I grabbed his wrist and tried to say "*Please*" through his hand.

He didn't open his eyes when he turned off and pocketed his phone with his free hand. Scrunching his face, he said, "I'm sorry. I'm really sorry..."

His shaky, wild eyes looked somewhere else as his hand went for my neck.

Now, I screamed. I fought. I tried to bite. I squirmed. I balled my hands into fists, but nothing seemed to hurt him. He squeezed. I couldn't breathe!

And then I saw Mr. Fuzzypants.

Mr. Fuzzypants?!

Mr. Fuzzypants jumped and *thunk*ed against Mr. Murray's head again and again. Tufts of white fur floated away, like dandelion fluff, with each *thud*.

"Get offa my sister!"

Mercedes?

Blood dripped down Mr. Murray's face and onto me. He let me go and spun around. In my blurry vision, I saw the blue and white flowers of Mercedes's tea-party dress.

I could breathe!

I sucked in all the breath I could, even though the air scraped all the way down my throat. I sucked it in as much as I could, then I blew out and sucked it all in again.

Everything in the garage snapped back into focus so quickly I got dizzy.

Mercedes hit Mr. Murray's head again with Mr. Fuzzypants. This time, Mr. Murray fell to the ground. She threw the hard, dead rabbit at Mr. Murray and scooped me up, like a knight rescuing a princess, and ran out of the garage. I wrapped my arms around her neck, unable to stop crying.

"Freeze!"

"Stop!" Two police officers blocked our way holding guns. I hadn't heard a siren. 911 got my message!

Mercedes shrieked. "Don't hurt my sister!" Her arms wrapped tighter around my body. I know she didn't *mean* to hurt me more.

"No one's going to hurt your sister," one of the police said gently. "We're here to help."

"I don't wanna go to jail and fry in the chair!" Mercedes started backing away. I could feel her body tremble, and I was afraid she'd drop me or crush me. Neither was a good option.

"It's not her!" I tried to shout, but my voice scratched like I'd swallowed a porcupine. I let go with one hand and pointed up our driveway. "In the garage. He tried—he tried…" I started coughing.

The two cops looked at each other. At that point, Mr. Murray was, in fact, staggering out of the garage. When he saw the two officers, he looked like a rabbit about to run, but they turned their guns on him.

"Stay right there," said the other cop to him.

Then, squealing around the corner, came Miss Carrie's car. She slammed on her brakes, part on our driveway, part on our neighbor's tree belt, and part still on the road. She left her car door open as she ran to us.

I'd never been so happy to see Miss Carrie in all my life!

"Portia! Mercedes! Oh my God!"

"Excuse me, ma'am, who are you?" The closer police officer stepped between her and us.

"I'm their nanny," she said, standing tall. "Mercedes called me and said there was an emergency and I needed to come right away."

Mercedes, still carrying me, shouldered by the officer and ran into Miss Carrie's arms—enough proof of her statement, it seemed.

Assured we were fine for the moment, the two cops put handcuffs on Mr. Murray. I was sobbing, and so was Mercedes. Miss Carrie holding us seemed to make even more tears fall from our eyes.

The ambulance arrived shortly. Dad…dad was taken out of the cellar with a sheet over him. I knew what that meant, and so did Mercedes. It took all of Miss Carrie's strength and the help of a police officer to hold my sister. And it took all of the lady police officer's strength to hold me. Both of us wanted to run after him and tear off the sheet and make him wake up.

The only thing I wouldn't do, though, was drink some tea.

*M*iss Carrie's face was fixed with her "You listen to me" look, which was making the police officer on his cell phone squirm as he glanced between me on the hospital bed, Miss Carrie and Mercedes in plastic chairs, and his note pad. We were the only ones in the tiny room, and the policeman had closed the door "for privacy."

"Yes, ma'am," he was saying to whoever was on the other side. "Walczak and Palecki are bringing Paguero in…" Paguero was the guy Mr. Murray had been talking to on the phone. The guy who had told him to kill me. "…and the car's been brought in as evidence. No, we don't have the street value of the drugs yet, and CSI hasn't found anything on the interior…"

I chewed the inside of my cheek to keep from talking. It felt weird, because the medicine they gave me took away almost all the pain. And I'd had to wait to get pain medicine to see if I had any "tea"— which I now knew were drugs, the bad kind—left in my system. I knew something was wrong with the tea, but I hadn't expected *that*…and thinking about *that* was even weirder than the not-pain I felt chewing my cheek to keep quiet.

Miss Carrie had called a lawyer while we were heading to the hospital and, like Mom and Dad, she'd told us not to say a word. I could see Mercedes biting her bottom lip hard as she rocked in the super-uncomfy-looking chair. I remember Mom had cleaned out the whole inside of the car before she'd even started working on the engine, telling me I couldn't even come into the garage because it was so filthy and the chemicals she was using weren't safe for kids. When she finally started working on the engine, and letting me be her "assistant mechanic" again, the whole inside was clean and smelled like new leather.

"…but between the call and Murray's testimony, that's still enough to bring in Paguero for questioning on both the Kessig homicide and that whole mess last August. It could be just the break we need."

I pressed my lips together. Were they going to open a Cartwright homicide case too? For Mom and Dad? Or were both really accidents, like Mr. Murray claimed? What would that mean for Mercedes?

Miss Carrie cleared her throat. I glanced at her and winced, hoping that I would never be on the other side of the glare she was giving to the officer, who was squirming even more as he scribbled—totally avoiding looking at all of us.

Even as he ended his call with a "Thank you, Captain, Ma'am. I'll keep you posted."

Miss Carrie stood up and took a step toward him. "Are you all set with us now?"

"I'm sorry, ma'am, but both girls—"

"Portia is not only under age, but under doctor's care right now. And you need a judge to state whether or not Mercedes qualifies as a witness. Furthermore, they have *just lost their father.*" She hissed that last part between her teeth, like she didn't think we'd hear. We did. Even with all the pain medicine, even though we'd seen the paramedics carry his sheet-covered body out of the basement, the words still felt like they stabbed me in the heart. Mercedes, too. She whimpered and squeaked her chair right next to the bed and me. Miss Carrie continued to lay into the officer. "Neither of the girls are saying anything until the doctor clears us and we speak with our lawyer. What, exactly, else do you need from us right now?"

With that, the officer left, kind of looking like a dog with its tail between its legs.

When the doctor came in and discharged me from the hospital, I was relieved Miss Carrie offered to take us to her home. I felt even better when she said we could stay as long as we liked. She'd take care of any paperwork to make that happen and keep us safe and together.

At least, I hoped it would work out that way. All I had left was my sister, and all she had left was me. Our parents, and even the dumb bunny, were all dead and gone.

I really did hope Mr. Fuzzypants found himself in a proper Bunny Heaven. With lots of hay-tea and carrot cake, rainbows every day, and sweet grass growing everywhere.

I guess he really was a good bunny.

Acknowledgements

As always, first and foremost, immeasurable thanks to my husband, Scott, for putting up with all the craziness of being married to an author. Not only do you "put up with it," but you are wonderfully supportive—even when it comes to applying your superior Google-Fu skills to looking up the effects of illegal drugs. Also, you do very well with being a bunny-daddy! I love you.

Right up there, many thanks to my family for always being supportive of me—even though what I write is not your usual reading material. I love you all!

I also want to give some extra special thanks to my Southbridge writers group. We started off as "Common Ground" and now we've just adjusted it to "Thai Writers" for the awesome restaurant we meet at—Extra, extra thank you to Sery and family! You guys had the most say and input of all my beta readers on Mr. Fuzzypants, and you've been there for me through so much of my writing career. You guys rock, and *thank you* so much.

Roxanne, Nanette, Kristi – thank you all for your feedback and edits! Rich Storrs, thank you for your last-minute rescue edits and being so thorough and demanding me to do better, as you always are! And Bracken, I bet you didn't expect a thank you, but I'm sending you one anyway because your feedback was also extremely helpful and the way you presented something gave me particular "fix" idea.

Kelly A. Harmon and Pole to Pole publishing, thank you for finding another of my stories good fit. I'm very happy to be working with you again!

And finally, thank you to all my friends and readers for buying a copy of *Tea with Mr. Fuzzypants*.

Author Bio

Trisha J. Wooldridge has been a freelance editor, copywriter, journalist, and author for over thirteen years. She's edited over forty books, three online courses, four tutoring manuals, several issues of *Massachusetts Horse* magazine, mutual fund resource information, and the text for the *Dungeons & Dragons: Stormreach*, a massive multi-player online role playing game. As a journalist, she's reviewed restaurants, wine, beer, and whiskey; she's covered international food trade and controversy over migrant tomato workers; and she's spotlighted over two dozen horsewomen and horse rescues throughout Massachusetts.

Her work includes over a dozen short stories and poems, including pieces in the EPIC award-winning *Bad-Ass Faeries* anthologies and the Stoker award-nominated New England Horror Writer anthologies. Under the name T.J. Wooldridge, she's published three middle grade novels: *The Kelpie, The Earl's Childe,* and *Silent Starsong.* As the writer half of a comic team, she creates, markets, and scripts for the vampire webcomic *Aurelio.* She is the former president of Broad Universe, as well as a member of New England Horror Writers, the Horror Writers Association, and the Society of Children's Book Writers & Illustrators. Find out more at http://www.anovelfriend.com.

Praise for *The Story of Noichi the Blind*

The novella's early fairy-tale tone gives way to a creeping, perverse darkness that grows through several ingenious twists to a bitterly ironic ending. To be honest, I enjoyed this more than I have most Hearn stories. Imagine Takashi Miike's version of *Snow White* and you're almost there.

– RUE MORGUE

Williamson's dark Japanese fairy tale, with its graphic scenes of supernatural horror, makes even the unexpurgated Grimms' stories seem tame.

– Publisher's Weekly

As readers of Richard Parks' "Yamabushi" surely cherish knowing, a *tengu* is a Japanese demon that delights in destroying saints. In this faux-found imitation of Lafcadio Hearn's Japanese supernatural pieces, there is a *tengu* much viler and ghastlier than Parks' creation. It isn't the worst thing in the tale. This extraordinary performance makes such comparably transgressive writing as the Marquis de Sade's seem totally crude.

– Booklist

Other books by Chet Williamson

A Step Across (w/Laurie Williamson)
Ash Wednesday
Defenders of the Faith
Dreamthorp
Hunters
Lowland Rider
McKain's Dilemma
Murder, Old and New (w/Laurie Williamson)
Reign
Robert Bloch's Psycho: Sanitarium
Second Chance
Soulstorm